THE COLONY

GRAVESIDE READS VOL. 1
BOOK 4

D.L. WINCHESTER

For A.R. and Rob, who insisted this story needed to be told.

THE COLONY

"You can't do this to me! I'm a mother! I was only trying to feed my children!"

I turned my head away from the woman sitting across the aisle from me. The bus continued its journey down the uneven road, a remnant of the time when this small town in what used to be East Tennessee thrived, before the Yellowstone eruption drove its residents to the coast. Now it, like so many other areas across the former United States, had been claimed by a group trying to escape the ghosts of civilization.

"The Colony," they called it. A religious oasis in the foothills of the Appalachian Mountains. The first prophet had established it soon after the aftershocks ended, leading a small group of survivors to establish a utopia built on the King James Bible and the Prophet's divine revelations.

Now the fourth prophet was in power, a charismatic leader who wanted to grow the population while weeding out troublemakers. He called it his "Holy mission from God."

The gate at the front of the bus squeaked as it opened, and the woman's screams got louder. A guard, dressed in military fatigues and carrying a nightstick, was walking down the aisle while his partner stood at the gate.

"No! Please! No!"

The guard jabbed a needle in her arm, and she slumped, unconscious, to the floor. *Can't kill the prisoners yet,* I thought. *The Prophet needs examples to punish.*

We'd been sentenced to death, but none of the other prisoners knew what would happen when we reached the old factory north of town. The guards would herd us off the bus and into cells. There, we would be given a last meal of cornmeal mush and have a chance to write to the prophet, begging for mercy. Then we'd shower and change into clean clothes, the hangman would weigh us, and we'd wait for midnight.

One at a time, the guards would lead us onto the old production floor. Our name and crimes would be read for the video camera recording our last moments, then the hangman would strap our arms and legs, put a hood over our heads, position the noose, and pull the lever.

Tomorrow, pictures of us will appear in the Colony's newspaper, along with lists of our crimes. The Prophet will explain that we were sinners, stains on the Colony, and our deaths were necessary to protect the righteous from the dangers of sin. By then, our bodies will have been cremated and the ashes dumped in the river.

I knew this, because I knew the Hangman.

He was my father-in-law.

When my wife got sick, he begged me not to look across the mountains for help.

Medicine was blasphemy, a lack of faith. But watching her suffer, I had to do something. He begged me to consider what she would live through if I was caught, having to endure her last days without me. But I was determined, and one foggy morning I slipped into the mountains, beginning the journey south to the Qualla Boundary, as the Eastern Cherokee called their reservation. They still had support from what was left of the government, and the doctors there were happy to pass on what they could.

By the time I returned, it was too late for the medicine to do my wife any good. She was in the final stages of her illness, and all the medicine would do was prolong her suffering. But as I watched her slip away, I realized even if I couldn't help her, I could help others. Those in the Colony who trusted science more than the prophet relied on expensive smugglers to bring in medicines and other luxuries. But I felt it would honor my wife's memory to bring comfort to others, as I tried to do for her.

I spent ten years running medicines, ten years of crossing the mountains to safety, then returning as a traitor.

They finally caught me by accident.

I had one more ridge to cross when I saw a fire on the road ahead. Normally, if I saw something like that, I'd avoid it, but the fire was in the only safe pass for two days in either direction, and a child was waiting for the medicine in my pack.

I crept through the trees, knowing it was either a fool or a Colony search party. When I reached the pass, I saw two men sitting by the fire with their backs to me. I was about to crawl into the open when a gun cocked.

"Well, hello there," a voice whispered. "Lost in the woods, are we?"

I cursed inwardly. It was damn foolish of me to think they'd all be out in the open for me to see. "Something like that."

"Nonsense. Put your hands behind your back." The cold metal handcuffs

tightened around my wrists. "We thought we'd catch one traitor tonight. Turns out we get two. The prophet will be pleased."

By the fire, one of the men undid a sleeping roll and laid down, while the other walked toward where we were hidden. He nodded into the dark, then turned back. I felt a stinging pain, and rubbed the spot.

"Just something to help you sleep."

I woke up in a cell at the old courthouse. A fat man in a constable's uniform was watching me, grinning.

"I do love when we catch a blasphemer, and today we got us two of 'em!"

On the cell's other bed, a young man sat up. "Where am I?"

"Jail, you scum. You tried your hand at smuggling, but your partner was a bounty hunter."

"Damn it."

He laughed. "Boys, you're gonna hang, but you don't have to hang alone. Just tell us who hired you, who the other sinners are."

I sat silent as my cell mate opened his mouth. "Deacon Malvern and his wife. Her mother is ill, and prayer isn't helping."

The constable grinned. Putting a deacon in the noose would be a feather in his cap.

"And what about you?" he asked me. "Whose lack of faith put you behind these bars?"

"My own."

He leaned in, pressing his face against the bars. "I'm sure they paid you well for your silence, but you can't spend that money in Hell."

"I wasn't paid. It was a personal trip."

He took a paper off his desk and read it. "In your pack, we found five vials of flu vaccine, two vials of tetanus, three vials of morphine, thirty syringes, two vials of epinephrine, three courses of radiation, and ten bottles of aspirin. If that's all for you, you should be dead by now."

"I guess I'm lucky."

He shook his head. "Not anymore, you ain't."

Ten of us went to trial the next morning. The judge was one of the deacons, a stern black man named Gardner. I'd run drugs for him, as I had for many of the deacons. But he would deny knowing me, even if I screamed his sins to the court.

I wouldn't, of course. My drugs had saved two of his grandchildren. No matter what the man had to do in public to survive, fingering him for his sins would serve no one.

My trial was short. The bounty hunters told Gardner where I'd been captured and what was in my pack, and the constable told him I'd confessed. I didn't say anything. There was nothing to say. Gardner ordered me to stand.

"Having reviewed the evidence and your lack of a defense, I find you guilty of the sin of Blasphemy. Under the authority granted this court, I sentence you to be taken from here to a place of execution and hung by the neck until dead. May God have mercy on your soul." He banged his gavel, and two guards led me out of the courtroom.

We arrived. The old part of the factory, the warehouse section, was crumbling, but the new addition, where the hangings took place, still stood. The guards herded us off the bus and into the building, where we were led into cells. I was last in line, and the guards pushed me into the cell closest to the white door that lead to the gallows.

Mush is mush, and my new clothes were a faded jumpsuit with a large stain in the crotch. At least the shower was warm. They didn't have to give us that luxury. I was lying on the cot when one of the guards appeared with pens and paper.

The request for mercy.

Everyone sentenced to death has the right to appeal to the Prophet. Of course, I knew the Prophet never saw the letters. The hangman reviewed them, and in a small number of cases granted mercy on behalf of the Prophet. If one was chosen tonight, the Prophet will include a statement in tomorrow's paper sharing how God led him to see that mercy for one of us was part of his divine providence.

It's horseshit, but a little bit of mercy keeps people believing in the prophet's goodness. I picked up the pen and looked at the blank page. I'd known one day I would have to write this letter, but I still hadn't figured out what to say. Most wrote long texts proclaiming sorrow for their sins and declaring that if forgiven, they would never sin again. But I knew that was bullshit.

I also knew who I was writing to.

With that in mind, I started.

Dear Jack,

Ten years ago you told me I'd end up here, and

now you can say, 'I told you so.' Bounty Hunters picked me up two days ago, and tonight I will die by your hand.

I suppose I should apologize. I don't believe either of us wanted it to end like this, but my stubborn devotion to helping others brought me here. I couldn't save your daughter, but I've saved hundreds since we held her hand as she breathed her last. I think that's what she would have wanted, but I'd give each of their souls to the devil himself for another day with her.

I'm sorry we're here, Jack, but I know what you have to do. There is no hate in my heart, just the satisfaction of having lived my last ten years in a way that would have made my wife proud.

Sincerely,

Your son-in-law,

Andrew

The guard returned and took my letter, and I sat on my cot to wait. Soon Jack would come in to weigh me, a necessary step to ensure a quick death. Hangmen before him had trusted the task to their assistants, but Jack was a perfectionist who wanted to handle it himself.

He didn't want someone dancing alive on the end of the rope because the drop didn't break their neck, or worse, to have someone decapitated by too long of a drop.

I heard something at the far end of the cell block, then a woman shrieking. "This is unnecessary, I am the wife of a Deacon!

I will be pardoned! You don't need to weigh me like a common sinner!"

I chuckled. One of the only rules about mercy was Jack could not extend it to Deacons or their families. The Prophet didn't want to be seen as playing favorites. Someone in this group might be extended mercy, but it wouldn't be her.

It took some time for the other nine to be weighed, but finally Jack came to my cell door.

It had been ten years since I'd seen him, but he looked to have aged twenty. He still had fire in his eyes though, reminding me of my wife.

"Hello Andrew."

"Hello, Jack."

He stood for a moment, looking at me. "You're well."

"For another few hours, at least."

He chuckled. "I suppose you're right." He passed a bathroom scale through the bars.

"Weigh yourself for me."

I put the scale on the floor and stepped onto it. "One fifty-eight," I read.

"Set the drop at six feet, two and a half inches," he muttered as he scribbled on his clipboard.

"You ready?" I asked.

"No." He sighed. "I've always known what you were doing. Those in power feared you because you did your job out of love, not for money. You'd be surprised how many runners are paid by the government to control the number of 'miracles.' But they knew they couldn't control you. So every 'miracle' you gave some poor family was one they couldn't give to a deacon's family member."

"Do they realize who I am?"

He shrugged. "I don't know that they ever knew who you were, just the fruits of your efforts. They'll eventually realize you're gone, but that could be a year from now, when the supplies you've brought in start to run out."

"Maybe someone else will fill my shoes."

"One can hope." He checked his watch. "An hour and a half until midnight. You're last on the schedule."

"I'll be dead no matter where I am on the schedule."

He stopped for a second, then sighed. "Thank you for trying to save my daughter. You loved her more than I ever could."

"We both loved her. We just chose different ways to express it."

***

The single mother was the first one taken through the white door. She was quiet, apparently still feeling the sedative they had given her on the bus. Five minutes after the door closed, I heard the clang of the trap.

Next was the deacon, followed by the runner he'd hired. Then his wife was dragged to the gallows.

"Call the Prophet!" she screamed. "I am a faithful servant! He doesn't realize I am here, he will pardon me! Call him! Call him!"

Five minutes later, the clang of the trap signaled her death.

Two pairs of adulterers were followed by another thief, and then it was my turn.

Through the white door and up the steps, where Jack would be waiting.

CLANG!

The sound startled me. I knew it had been an accident of some kind. I began pacing in my cell, willing the moments to pass, but time seemed to stand still. Finally, a single guard emerged from the white door and unlocked my cell.

"You are free to go."

"What? Where's Jack?"

"Jack is dead."

I sank onto the cot. "What?"

The guard shook his head. "He put the noose around his neck and told us he would die in your place. Crazy thing to do, if you ask me. Before we could stop him, he'd pulled the trap and hung himself."

I sat there, stunned. "Did he say anything else?"

"Only to give you this." He handed me a folded note.

Dear Andrew,

When you read this, I will be dead.

Death comes for all of us, and my time has come. One of the radiation treatments you were carrying on your last journey was for me. Without it, I would have died within a month.

I will tell the guards I am dying for you, but I am dying to prove I have the courage you have always shown. I cannot do what you have done, but by dying in your place, maybe you will be able to continue your work.

Godspeed, Andrew.

Your Friend,

Jack.

PART II
A NEED FOR HOME

Two miles north of the execution building was a bridge over the river. I walked across it and followed old roads along the north bank until I reached a village called Del Rio. The northlands were sparsely populated; the colony didn't need the land. A few hunters worked up there, bringing wild game back to the colony.

It had taken me most of the day to walk to Del Rio, and it was sunset when I slipped into the back yard of Nurse Holm's house. She was one of three nurses I carried medicine for, and the only one I trusted. Dennie Holm had cared for my wife in her last days, telling me what medicines would save her and staying by her side while I made the attempt to get to the Indian reservation.

I'd arrived home too late to save my wife, but the medicine had saved the life of a child.

For a while, I blamed myself for not making the trip faster, but I learned that was ridiculous. The mountains were unforgiving, and trying to push myself was a good way to not make it back at all.

Quietly, I slipped onto Dennie's porch and knocked on the

door, ducking into the shadows. The door opened with a pistol pointing out.

"Who is it?" Dennie hissed.

"It's me," I said.

She stepped out and turned toward me, gun still in hand. "I heard you were hanged."

"They were going to hang me. Jack hanged himself in my place."

She paused for a moment, then cocked the gun. "How do I know there aren't a bunch of Colony officers waiting out there to arrest me?"

"Dennie, you know I wouldn't do that."

"I don't know nothing. I don't trust no one either. You know how long it takes news to get out here from town. I didn't know they captured you until this afternoon. Hughie Crawford said they were going to hang you last night."

"They didn't. They let me out this morning, and I walked all day to get here because you're the only person I trust." I softened my voice. "Jack said one of the medications on my last run was for him. You're the only nurse he would trust."

She studied me for a moment, then lowered the gun as a scream came from inside the house.

"What's that?"

"Girl giving birth. Come help me."

I followed her inside, watching her slide the gun into a holster at the small of her back. She'd converted two rooms into hospital wards. There were four beds in this room, but only one was occupied.

The woman was in her thirties, but to Dennie, that was young enough to be a girl. No one was with her, which wasn't unusual. Everyone knew Dennie used medicines, and if she was raided, you didn't want to be caught there. If you weren't there, you could play dumb when the Colony officers came calling.

"She's got no one. They hanged her husband six months ago. He tried to kill the Prophet, but failed."

I nodded. I remembered the attempt. The fool had taken a kitchen knife and broken into the Prophet's house intending to stab him, but the Prophet hadn't been home that night.

His guards had found the man, and two days later he was hanged.

"Do exactly what I say," Dennie said. "The baby doesn't want to come, and I may have to cut her to get it out. Since you got caught, I don't have anything to ease the pain."

Dennie didn't have to cut her, but it was a close thing. The baby was in a small crib next to the mother, who was fast asleep. She looked familiar, but I couldn't place her.

"You don't remember, do you?" Dennie asked. "She was your wife's best friend. Rose Huntley."

Realization struck. Rose. She and my wife had been inseparable. I wondered why I hadn't realized it was her, but ten years and the agony of childbirth didn't help.

The baby started to cry, and I picked it up, bouncing gently to soothe it.

"I wish Haley had gotten to see you do that."

I looked down at the bed to find Rose looking up at me.

"I do too," I said, as Dennie left the room.

"You two loved each other so much. It's wrong, how little time you had."

"I agree."

She chuckled. "My fool husband, on the other hand..."

"I heard what happened to him."

"He wanted to be a hero. He wanted the world to know who

he was, so he tried to kill the Prophet. I told him it wouldn't work. I told him not to, but he needed to do it."

"I don't understand that need, the desire for attention."

She smiled. "You wouldn't. You've spent the last ten years doing everything you can to avoid attention. If you get noticed, you die. Ray thought if he got noticed, we'd be living large."

"Right now, there's a part of me that wishes he'd succeeded. I'm tired of being needed. I'm tired of seeing people die because we're too foolish to see that medicine is not an affront to God, but a gift from him."

"Maybe you should be the next Prophet."

I laughed. "The Deacons would never choose me."

"That was Ray's plan. He thought if he killed the Prophet, the Deacons would have no choice but to make him the next Prophet."

"Foolish," was all I could say. The baby started screaming. "I think she's hungry."

"Probably."

I handed the baby to her, then stepped out of the room to give Rose some privacy.

The next morning, Dennie was waiting for me in the kitchen when I came down for breakfast. "Can you cross the mountain for me?"

I stood there for a moment. I'd just escaped death after being caught crossing the mountain, and now she wanted me to do it again.

"I wouldn't ask if I didn't need it, Andy. I know you just got caught, but you're still the best there is, and quite frankly, you're the best hope for some of the sick people around here."

I nodded. I wasn't afraid to cross the mountain, especially not from Del Rio. I could follow the old roads through Cataloochee, far from where the bounty hunters patrolled. But after Jack's death, during the walk here from the prison, I had started to wonder if I was really doing any good with my work. No matter how many runs I made, people still died, and they would keep dying.

Dennie sat down at the table with me and put her hand on mine. "You're thinking about Jack, aren't you?"

"Somehow, the world was better knowing he was in it. Now that he's gone, I don't really know how to respond."

She sighed. "I don't like to speak for the dead. But I think he died so you could keep saving others."

What she said made sense. And Jack's death would be for nothing if I stopped working.

"Honestly, Dennie, I'm at a point in my life where I want something to come back to. Seeing Rose hold her baby last night, it made me realize I'm not getting any younger. I've spent ten years going over the mountain, and if something happened to me, who would notice? Who would care?"

"I would. The patients would. But I know that's not enough." She smiled, a playful grin that suggested she knew something I didn't. "Maybe you should go see Rose before you leave."

"My wife's best friend?" I shook my head. "I'm not sure that's a good idea."

"Andy, it's been ten long years. You both need someone, and that little girl needs a father."

I nodded again. "I'll think about it."

Dennie rolled her eyes. "Go talk to her, Andy. You'll never let yourself do it if all you do is think."

I sat down on the bed next to Rose. The baby was asleep in her arms.

"What did you decide to name her?" I asked.

"Audrey," she replied with a smile. "I know that was the name Haley always wanted to use, so I thought it would honor her."

A tear rolled down my cheek. "I think it's perfect."

"I was always jealous of Haley. She had you. Tall, dark, unflappable you. Meanwhile I bounced from guy to guy and finally ended up with a fool."

I didn't know how to respond to that. Was I really worth the envy? Hell, dating and relationships hadn't even crossed my mind since losing Haley. It couldn't. My life was on the line every time I crossed the mountains; having someone waiting for me back in the colony would be leverage against me.

Being loved was a luxury I'd denied myself to sacrifice for others.

"Life ain't fair sometimes," I finally managed.

"I know. But these past ten years, sometimes I'd be lying alone in bed wondering what you were up to. I'd wonder if you were as lonely as I was. But then some other guy would start talking to me, and things would be okay for a while, until they weren't. Then it was back to wondering about you."

I sighed, then looked at her. She laughed. "I know it's kind of weird, I mean, you literally saw me give birth last night and now I'm telling you I want to be with you. But sometimes you have to take advantage of the opportunities you're given."

I stood up, then leaned over her bed and kissed her softly on the lips. I hadn't kissed anyone since Haley died, and it brought back memories of those kisses, but there was also something different, something that sparked deep in my soul. It was almost a reawakening, a realization I could love again.

———

Two days later, we walked down the road toward the mountains, Audrey comfortable in Rose's arms, and me carrying everything else Dennie had sent with us, along with a list of needed supplies.

Rose lived in an old church on the banks of a small creek. It was one of the only buildings in the area that had survived the Yellowstone eruption unscathed. She let us in, and after putting Audrey in a small crib, she came and sat next to me on the couch.

"So you're going over the mountains?"

"For Dennie. She's the only one I'll run for now."

She laid her head on my shoulder. "I don't want you to go, but I know it's important."

I put my arm around her. "I want to stay here."

"You can't though. You have to go get the medicine and save people. It's what you do, and I wouldn't want to change that." She leaned up and kissed me gently, then winced. "Damn. Giving birth hurts like hell."

"I wouldn't know."

She elbowed me playfully. "Get out of here. The sooner you go, the sooner you'll be home."

It was different, knowing Rose and Audrey were waiting for me to return. My route took me up the old forest road past Max Patch, then down into Harmon's Den and across the Pigeon River, up past Buzzard's Roost and along the old trails on the ridge of Mount Sterling, then finally down the old highway from Newfound Gap to the Qualla Boundary. I wasn't reckless.

There were faster routes, and there were more dangerous routes. My route balanced my desire for speed with solid, safe paths deep in the wilderness away from the bounty hunters.

Two weeks after I left, I walked up the road toward Rose's old church. A storm had blown through, slowing me down and turning the trails to slushy mud. My pack was full, and I thought about going straight to Dennie's, but a bigger part of me wanted to see Rose.

She was sitting on the front steps when I approached. When she saw me, she got up and ran toward me.

"Hey there," I called cheerfully, then I saw the look on her face. "What's the matter?"

"Dennie is dead."

"Oh my God." I took her hand and led her inside. Audrey was in her crib, kicking joyfully, and she stopped to look at me when I came in. I sat on the couch with Rose and took her hand. "What happened?"

"It was a week ago. The Colony Patrol came and arrested her. Apparently a little boy was bitten by a rattlesnake, and had an allergic reaction to the antivenom. She did everything she could, but the allergic reaction was too strong. He died, and his grandfather reported her for using medicine to try to save him."

I exhaled sharply. "Who was it?"

"A deacon named Gardner."

Leon Gardner. The same deacon who sentenced me to death for bringing medicine into the colony. A deacon whose entire family had benefited from Dennie's work and the medicines I brought her.

Everyone knew who the nurses were, even the Deacons and the Prophet. The problem was finding someone to bear witness against them. There was an unwritten code that no one would bear witness against a nurse, even if they made a mistake or couldn't save a loved one.

Gardner had violated that code.

I kissed Rose, then stood.

"I have an errand to run," I said, hoping I didn't sound as angry as I felt.

"Gardner's dead too, Andy. They found him in his barn two days after Dennie was hanged. He shot himself."

I sank back onto the bed, and she pressed her body against mine. "I'm sorry you came home to such bad news. The whole time you were gone, I wished you were here with us."

I smiled, in spite of the circumstances, and pulled her close for a kiss. "I wanted to be here too," I whispered.

We laid there, snuggled against each other, as the sun went down. Rose fell asleep, quietly snoring next to me, but I couldn't sleep.

Every time I closed my eyes, I saw Dennie Holm swinging in the noose I'd escaped.

I woke up to find Rose's arms around me. I'd lost count of the number of times this had happened in the month since I'd returned from my last trip over the mountain.

"You didn't sleep well," she whispered, rubbing my back. I was still getting used to having someone to support me. After ten years of keeping it all bottled up inside, every emotion, memory, and problem, suddenly being able to set them loose felt more freeing than walking away from my execution.

"I'll be okay." I didn't know if that was the truth.

She pulled me tight to her. We were about the same size, something I had come to appreciate over the last month, as I woke in the night with cold sweats or tossed and turned as the dreams haunted me.

I rolled over to face her. She was beautiful, not in the way Haley had been beautiful.

Haley had been a wisp, a quiet girl with a rail thin body and stern features. Rose was not fat, but she was filled out and soft, with a round face and wavy brown hair. I ran my hand along her cheek and she smiled.

"You're angry, aren't you? You don't want to be angry, but you can't escape it."

I nodded. She was learning to read my emotions quickly, since we rarely spent time with anyone but ourselves. "Two people I loved are dead, and while neither one was my fault, I still want some sense of vengeance."

She looked to the corner, where my rifle leaned, and I saw the fear in her eyes.

"I'm not going to do anything foolish."

"If you did it, I'm sure it wouldn't be," she said. "You would kill him and slip back into the shadows, not linger when your plan fell apart."

"I can't be that selfish now, not with you and Audrey to look after."

A tear came to her eye. "You care about us that deeply?"

I nodded. "I know I've only been here a month, but I've felt things I haven't felt since I lost Haley. I'm falling in love with you, Rose."

She smiled, and kissed me on the mouth, pushing me back into the bed and rolling on top of me.

"Those words," she whispered, "you better mean them."

"How could I not?"

She sat up and pulled off her shirt, exposing her swollen breasts. I smiled and caressed one. I'd seen them as she fed Audrey, but this was different. I felt a growing I hadn't felt in years, and Rose smiled as she found it with her hand.

Then the baby started crying.

I laughed and she smiled.

"Audrey has perfect timing," she said.

I pulled her down for another kiss. "If I'd known telling you how I felt would get a response like this..."

She rolled her eyes, then went to check on the baby.

"Andy!"

"What?" I got up and went to her. Audrey was coughing, and her face and neck were starting to swell. I recognized the symptoms; we'd seen them too many times in the colony now that no one was vaccinated. Just to be sure, I gently pried open Audrey's mouth and saw the gray mucus covering the back of her throat.

"Diphtheria," I said.

***

The nearest nurse was ten miles away over mountain roads. A day's journey in good conditions, with Rose and Audrey going with me. Even then, there was no guarantee they would have the medicine to treat her.

Rose sat nursing Audrey, the tears quietly rolling down her face, as I paced the floor.

"You're thinking of going over the mountain, aren't you?"

I nodded. "Are you up for the trip?"

"What do you mean?"

"I mean I'm scared, Rose. There's no guarantee Jean Norton will have the medicine we need to take care of Audrey, and even if she does, I don't want to raise her where we have to fear her death every time she coughs."

I'd fallen in love with the tiny baby, watching her big blue eyes looking up at me as I held her. She was learning to smile now, her mouth popping open in grins that seemed bigger than she was.

"You want us to go? To leave the colony?"

"What's holding us here besides fear of the unknown? Nothing is going to change. I could kill a hundred prophets, and the deacons will just raise another. I have something to live for, and I don't want to lose it because of a foolish way of life I stopped believing in long ago."

She smiled. "I'm with you, Andy. I'll follow you over the mountain if it means a chance at a better life for us."

Leaving wasn't complicated. I loaded our few possessions of value into a knapsack, and Rose created a sling for Audrey from a length of cloth. I picked up my rifle and the bag of medicine I had brought for Dennie on my last trip. I'd already checked it for the diphtheria medicine, but I would leave it with Jean. She would find a use for it, I was sure.

Our journey would start by heading through the mountains toward a place called Grassy Fork. A small group of settlers were there, and it was mostly safe from the Colony's influence, particularly if they disagreed with a policy. There were only a handful of entrances to the area, so they always knew when someone was approaching their village.

I'd never run for Jean—she had a group of local men who went over the mountain for her—but I knew her from passing through Grassy Fork on my way to Dennie's. She would help us, if she could.

We arrived at the small house near sunset. I could have made it in less time, but Rose wasn't in the same shape I was in. I left her in the woods a little ways up the road while I approached Jean's home and circled it, looking for any sign of problems. When I was convinced it was okay, I went back to Rose and we approached the house.

Jean was waiting for us on the front porch, shotgun in hand. When she saw me, she lowered it.

"You should know better than to sneak around here carrying a gun. One of my patients saw you and thought you was a Colony Officer or a bounty hunter."

"Just being careful after what happened to Dennie Holm," I explained, pulling Audrey from her wrap. "I've got a baby girl with diphtheria."

She sighed. "It's been going around. Ain't got no antitoxin, but I have a dose or so of antibiotics."

I handed her the bag of medicine. "I didn't see anything in here that would help Audrey, but I thought you could use it."

She eyed the bag with gratitude. "Bounty hunters keep catching my runners coming down Big Creek. I've lost two in the last three months."

"They caught me two months ago. I thought it was just bad luck."

Jean shook her head. "There's some rumors floating around that the Prophet has doubled the bounty on runners. They say he's sick, and he's using the confiscated medicine to try to heal himself. Only it ain't working. He's dying, and it might spark a war. There's two groups of deacons vying to choose the next prophet, and neither of 'em has enough support to get their man in office."

I nodded, silently understanding the consequences of a war among the deacons.

Without medicine, it would mean the slaughter of whoever they could convince to fight for them.

"I'm glad we're getting out then."

She cocked her head in agreement. "Give me a minute to give the baby this shot. If you're going through Big Creek, your best chance is to leave tonight."

I shook my head. "We're going to leave tomorrow, up the old gulf road."

"Ain't no road there anymore. Couple of landslides took it out. Washed fifty feet of road away."

"Oh." I looked at Rose, then at Audrey. Going through Big Creek would be infinitely more dangerous, but I didn't see much choice.

"I'll sedate the baby," Jean offered. "That will help with noise."

Rose nodded. She looked scared, but determined. I went to her and held her hand. "If you don't want to go, it's fine. I can be back with the medicine in less than three weeks."

"It might be too late by then," Rose protested. "We're with you, Andy, come hell or high water."

Bounty hunters were waiting for us on the bridge over the Pigeon River at Waterville. Not us in particular, but it was a natural choke point, and I could see three of them in the moonlight.

"Why are they out in the open?" Rose asked as I considered the situation. She was right. If they were waiting to ambush a runner, they'd be hiding, not standing in the open like that.

Then I heard a squawk, and figured it out.

"Radios. They've got watchers on the trails, so these boys have plenty of heads up when someone is coming."

I raised my gun, an old Henry Survival Rifle I'd picked up in a pawn shop on my last trip for Dennie. It was underpowered, shooting a .22 long rifle cartridge, but it got the job done against the small game I hunted for sustenance on the trails.

These three would test its limits.

I thought about slipping around to the east, past the old power plant, and trying to cross there, but I didn't dare in the dark.

"Stay here," I whispered to Rose. "If something happens to me, follow the old highway four miles that way," I pointed, "to the next village. Ask for Jed Harper."

She hugged me. "Be careful."

I slipped out of our hiding spot and crept across the bridge. The three men were at the rail with their backs to me. When I was a hundred feet away, I brought my rifle up, aiming for the biggest man's neck. That was the problem with the .22. It lacked stopping power for anything larger than, say, a squirrel. But it was what I had.

Fifty feet. Did I keep going and push my luck, or take my first shot? I crept closer. Forty feet, thirty, my finger tightened on the trigger and a bolt of flame shot from the gun.

Even in the dark, I could tell my bullet had torn through the man's neck, punching holes in the carotid arteries and the jugular veins as it went. His hands went to his throat, but I was already turning. The man on his right twisted toward me, but I hit him with three shots in the chest and he fell.

The last man was trying to draw his gun, but it was stuck. I didn't care. The gun fired, and he slumped to the ground. Only the big man was still standing, leaning on the rail trying to stop the blood squirting from his neck. I got the last man's gun loose and approached the big man.

His eyes went wide in terror, but only for a second. The pistol roared, and he fell dead. I checked the other two, but they were gone. I reloaded the rifle, then went through the dead men's pockets and came up with five extra magazines for the pistol.

"Are they dead?"

I spun to find Rose standing behind me. "That wasn't smart," I said, exhaling.

"I'm sorry."

"Yes, they're dead."

She nodded. I'd killed three men in front of her, and all she did was nod.

"Where to now?"

I pointed at a road leading up the hill. "I'd bet their buddies up the trail heard the shooting and are heading this way to investigate. This old road is the best way to avoid them."

With that, we disappeared into the dark.

At daybreak, we stopped to rest at the old Mt. Cammerer fire lookout. Rose nursed Audrey while I found my blanket, a survival model I had picked up on my last trip over the mountain.

I sat down next to Rose, and she rested her head on my shoulder.

"Twenty-four hours ago, I was going to make love to you. Now we're on our way to a new life."

I kissed the top of her head, and after Audrey finished, we drifted off leaning against each other.

Three days later, we had started our descent off the ridgeline when I heard a rustling in the bushes ahead of us. I stopped, Rose behind me, and waited.

A large black bear came out of the bushes and stopped in the middle of the trail, looking at us.

"Don't move," I whispered, slowly raising my gun.

Audrey screamed, and the bear turned away, heading down the hill. Rose and I looked at each other and laughed.

Audrey was trying to smile, but it was hard. The first day, she had improved, but once the antibiotic wore off, she slowly started getting worse. Her face was fully swollen, and I could see the back of her throat was gray. Her forehead was burning, and Rose was constantly feeding her, trying to keep her hydrated. By my reckoning, we could be at the Qualla Boundary by nightfall.

We were crossing a stream when I heard a splash behind me, and I turned to see Rose had slipped and fallen in the river. She got to her feet, unable to put weight on her right leg, and I helped her to the shore.

"Are you okay?"

The baby was screaming from the cold water, and Rose was wincing in pain.

"It's my ankle, I think I've broken it."

"That's not good."

She looked me in the eye. "Take Audrey and go, Andy. Come back for me if you can. But save her."

I shook my head. "I'm saving both of you."

She tried to smile. "What are you, a white knight?"

"An ugly hillbilly who doesn't want to give up the bestlooking thing in his life."

We stumbled into town two hours after dark. Anyone who saw us would have laughed, a baby on the back of a woman on the back of a man. I'd carried Rose the last three miles after the pain in her ankle had gotten to be too much.

It always struck me how different it was when you got to the Qualla Boundary. Lights stayed on all night, and cars ran up and down the roads. There were restaurants and stores, a prosperous life helped by the way the mountains behind us had blocked the ash from Yellowstone's explosion.

A cop saw us, and loaded us into his car for the trip to the hospital. Rose was exhausted and almost fell asleep during the trip while I clung to Audrey. She hadn't improved, but at least she wasn't doing worse.

We were shown into a room, and one doctor went to work on Audrey while another looked at Rose's ankle. Audrey's doctor came over to me.

"You're damn lucky, son. Another 24 hours, and your little girl would have been in real trouble."

"We got her here as fast as we could."

"I think she'll be okay. I don't like making promises, but I like her chances." He smiled at me. "Good on you for getting them out."

I felt myself relax. "We've actually met a few times. I used to run medicines across the mountains."

"I remember you, son. I remember most of the runners I've met. I admire the hell out of you, risking your life to make sure your people get some sort of care." He looked over at Rose, then at Audrey. "It looks like you've built a good life for yourself."

I caught Rose's eye and grinned. "I sure have."

The doctor working on Rose's ankle finished. "It's not broken, just a painful sprain. I've wrapped it to stabilize it, and if you try to walk you'll need a boot."

Rose nodded.

"Stay here, make yourself at home," Audrey's doctor said. "There's a couch and a bed, we'll take care of your little girl, and hopefully we can get you out of here soon."

As soon as they left, Rose curled her finger, beckoning me to the bed. I laid down next to her and put my arms around her.

"I know it's a little narrow," she whispered, "but I don't want you sleeping on that couch if there's room next to me." I kissed her, and looking into her eyes, I saw our future, away from the Colony, in the home that was each other's arms.

ABOUT THE AUTHOR

D.L. Winchester lives in the foothills of southern Appalachia. A former mortician, his work searches the darkness to find tales worth telling. He is the author of over three hundred obituaries, numerous short stories, the story collection Shadows of Appalachia, and the flash fiction collection A Terrible Place.

In his spare time, he can be found searching for inspiration in the world around him and trying to keep his children from becoming the next generation of horror villains.

facebook.com/writerdlwinchester

If you are a fan of horror stories and tales, you'll want to follow Undertaker Books.
We're bringing you stories to take to your grave.

www.ingramcontent.com/pod-product-compliance
Lightning Source LLC
Chambersburg PA
CBHW031551310726
48971CB00008B/2710